Tantrum Alert

Modra Ploogsik stared down at Blork. "Was this your doing?" she growled.

Blork felt embarrassed. His face got warm, and his cheeks turned dark green.

"Look at him blush!" whispered Rugrub. "He *must* be guilty!"

Modra Ploogsik appeared to be thinking the same thing.

"I *didn't* do it!" protested Blork. "I *like* Moomie Peevik!"

"Oooooh," shouted Appus Meko happily. "Blork likes Moomie Peevik!"

He began making slurpy kissing sounds against the back of his hand.

Blork started to tremble.

"Look out," whispered Mimsy Borogrove. "He's going to have a tantrum!"

Books by Bruce Coville

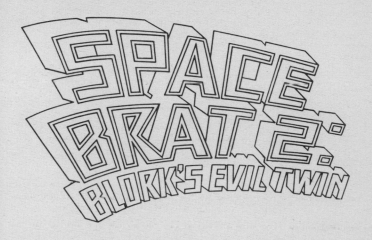

SPACE BRAT 2: BLORK'S EVIL TWIN

BRUCE COVILLE

Interior illustrations by
Katherine Coville

A MINSTREL® BOOK

PUBLISHED BY POCKET BOOKS

New York   London   Toronto   Sydney   Tokyo   Singapore

A MINSTREL PAPERBACK *ORIGINAL*

A Minstrel Book published by
POCKET BOOKS, a division of Simon & Schuster Inc.
1230 Avenue of the Americas, New York, NY 10020

Copyright © 1993 by Bruce Coville
Interior illustrations copyright © 1993 by Katherine Coville
Front cover illustration copyright © 1993 by Greg Wray

ISBN: 0-671-77713-0

First Minstrel Books printing August 1993

10   9

A MINSTREL BOOK and colophon are registered trademarks
of Simon & Schuster Inc.

Printed in the U.S.A.

for each other

Contents

1

INVENTIONS

"Hey, *Space Brat*—want a little breakfast?"

Blork turned just in time to see his enemy Appus Meko pull back a spoon and let go. A gob of sticky cereal flew through the air and hit Blork's forehead with a *splat!*

Blork's eyes bulged.

He began to shake and shiver.

Soon he looked as if he was going to explode.

"Tan-trum, tan-trum!" chanted the other kids. "Have a tantrum, Blork! Have a tantrum! Have a tantrum! Have a tantrum *now!*"

Blork didn't want to have a tantrum. He thought he had stopped doing that forever. But he was afraid he wouldn't be able to hold himself back. The old "tantrum feeling" that meant an explosion was coming was bubbling inside him.

Just as the tantrum was about to rip out of him, it was stopped by the tickley feeling of a long green tongue slurping the cereal from his face.

"Lunk!" giggled Blork. "Cut that out!"

Lunk was Blork's pet. He was a poodnoobie, which meant that he weighed three hundred and fifty pounds, had six legs, and was covered with purple fur. Also, he had three tongues. Right now he was licking Blork with the middle one, which was medium rough.

He took another slurp. It tickled. Blork smiled. Just having Lunk close made him feel better. Putting his hand on the poodnoobie's huge purple head, he whispered, "Thanks, pal. You kept me from blowing up!"

Lunk burped happily.

Lunk had been part of the adventure that earned Blork the name Space Brat. It started the day Blork brought the poodnoobie to school, where it got into so much trouble that the teacher, Modra Ploogsik, had called the Big Pest Squad and asked them to take Lunk away.

When Blork tried to rescue Lunk, the two of them had ended up escaping into outer space. During their adventures Blork learned to stop having the incredible tantrums that had made him the biggest brat on the planet Splat. That was why he had not had a tantrum for the last two weeks.

But not having tantrums wasn't easy when people like Appus Meko kept picking on him. Of course, Appus Meko picked on everyone. But in the last few days he had been concentrating on Blork.

Blork thought he knew why. Before he had

gone into space, it had been easy to send him into a screaming rage that the other kids found hilarious (as long as they had room to get away from him). Back then, the class had been able to count on him for a little amusement whenever things got boring.

Appus Meko resented the fact that Blork wasn't having tantrums anymore and kept trying to get him to have another one. He also resented the way the newsies had gone nuts over Blork's adventures. One of the reporters had labeled him "Space Brat," and there had been stories about him on the tube every night for a week.

Appus Meko hated seeing Blork get so much attention. Which explained why, in the last three days, he had pinged Blork's antennae, spilled dissolving powder on his homework, and dropped a gooby worm down his back. (Gooby worms are long and slimy and have hundreds of tickly legs.)

Blork had nearly had a tantrum over the worm, but Moomie Peevik had helped him get it out of his shirt and then talked quietly to him until he calmed down.

Blork was glad of the help. But he did not like the fact that it came from Moomie Peevik. He had always considered her a pain in the noseholes.

As Lunk finished licking the cereal from Blork's face, the Childkeeper rolled over. "Time to leave for school," it beeped.

Blork sighed and took Lunk back to his room. Jamming his computer into his backpack, he joined the other kids from the Block 78 Child House as they headed for school.

Blork's class had sixteen kids. Actually, this was true for every class on the planet Splat. The people who ran the schools figured that sixteen kids was as much as any grown-up should ever have to cope with.

Fifteen kids in Blork's class were from Splat. The sixteenth kid was Bob the Foreign Student, who came from another planet.

Blork felt sorry for Bob because he was so

funny-looking. After all, the poor kid had no antennae, and a big fleshy blob on his face where his noseholes should be. Privately, Blork thought of him as "Bob the Blob." But he never said that out loud because he knew it would hurt Bob's feelings.

"We have a special treat today," said Modra Ploogsik when the kids were all in their seats.

"We're going to blow up the school?" cried Appus Meko eagerly.

The other kids laughed. Modra Ploogsik started to get her cranky face.

Blork stared straight ahead. He was trying to be good, but his brain was filled with mischief. He kept thinking of pranks he could pull to make the others laugh the way Appus Meko just had. He reminded himself that when he used to pull pranks, usually someone had ended up crying.

Blork tried to forget about pranks and concentrate on what Modra Ploogsik was saying—something about a visit to the Museum of New Inventions.

Blork perked up. He loved inventions, and

people on Splat were always coming up with great ideas for new ones. His current favorite was rocket roller skates. They were not perfect yet; the people who were testing them kept crashing into things. But Blork was sure that as soon as the inventor figured out how to make them stop, they would be very popular.

Modra Ploogsik watched carefully as her class piled into the rocketbus to go to the museum. She had been keeping a close eye on Blork during the two weeks since he had returned from space. She still couldn't believe he wasn't the brat he had once been.

In the rocketbus Blork sat next to Brillig, the smartest kid in the class. Appus Meko sat behind them and kept trying to make Blork lose his temper, until Brillig finally turned around and told him to shut up.

Modra Ploogsik led the class into the museum. Blork began to smile. The place was filled with spiffy stuff.

Blork felt even happier when their guide chose *him* to try the Wall-Walker Shoes. He walked up one wall and across the ceiling. Only he hadn't bothered to fasten the tops, so he nearly fell out before he got to the other side.

"If you aren't careful, you'll sprain your antennae," whispered Moomie Peevik when he got back down.

Next the guide showed them a trap made to catch giant fuzzygrumpers.

"I bet it won't work," said Brillig.

Blork agreed. He had watched a show about giant fuzzygrumpers just the week before. They were the most ferocious creatures on the planet.

"Well, here's something that works, and I can prove it," said the guide. She led them to a case marked ATOMIC MINIATURIZER RAY GUN. "This can shrink things to one-tenth of their normal size. Here, I'll give you a demonstration."

Picking up the Miniaturizer, she pointed it at a chair and pulled the trigger.

Zaaaap! A purple ray struck the chair.

Soon the chair looked like a toy.

A hazy purple cloud floated above it.

"What's that?" asked Mimsy Borogrove, pointing to the cloud.

"I know!" cried Tovi, waving her hand. "I know! It's extra atoms. The Miniaturizer shrinks things by removing nine out of every ten atoms. I read about it in *Science Whiz Daily*."

"Very good," said the guide as she put the Miniaturizer back into its case. "Unfortunately, we have no way to restore those atoms. This device would be more useful if we could make things big again. But as it is, once shrunk, always shrunk. Walk this way. I want to show you our Fat Injector."

Appus Meko followed close behind her, copying the way she walked.

"Fat Injector?" asked Karpal, putting her hands on her stomach and looking worried. "What's that for?"

"To help people explore planets that don't have much gravity," said Brillig.

"Euuuww!" cried Karpal. "That is totally gross!"

The Fat Injector was a big machine, with lots of wires and a helmet. After examining it the class headed for the Solar-Powered Pocket Cookie Baker.

"You might call that a Fat Injector, too," joked Blork.

He meant to say it to Moomie Peevik, but suddenly he realized that she wasn't there. Then he heard her voice.

"Help!" she cried. "Someone get me out of here!"

Blork turned and gasped.

Moomie Peevik was stuck in the Fat Injector! She was getting bigger by the second, blowing up like a Moomie Peevik balloon.

"Someone get me out of this thing before I explode!" she screamed.

2

COPIER

Blork ran to the Fat Injector. Moomie Pee-vik was already so round that he couldn't stretch high enough to pull the helmet from her head. Grabbing the wall-walker shoes, he slipped into them. Then he walked up the side of the Fat Injector and knocked the helmet off Moomie Peevik's head.

Instantly she stopped expanding.

"My hero," she said.

Blork made a face.

Two people from the museum came run-

ning over. "What on Splat is going on here?" asked one of them.

"No time for that now!" cried the other. "We've got to get this kid to the Liposuction Room fast! Come on, let's roll!"

Flipping Moomie Peevik onto her side, they began rolling her toward the door like a giant beach ball. "Don't worry," said one of them. "We'll have you back to normal by this afternoon."

"Wait!" called Karpal. "Take me! I have some fat that needs to get sucked out, too."

"Sorry," said the guide. "The Liposuction Room is only for major emergencies."

"Darn!" muttered Karpal.

Modra Ploogsik was furious. "I want to know who did this!" she said. "And I want to know *now!*"

"Blork unplugged her," said Appus Meko. "So he must have been closest to her when it happened."

Modra Ploogsik stared down at Blork. "Was this your doing?" she growled.

Blork's face got warm. His cheeks turned dark green.

"Look at him blush!" whispered Rugrub. "He *must* be guilty!"

Modra Ploogsik appeared to be thinking the same thing.

"But I *didn't* do it!" protested Blork. "I *like* Moomic Peevik!"

"Oooooh!" shouted Appus Meko happily. "Blork likes Moomie Peevik!"

He began making slurpy kissing sounds against the back of his hand.

Blork started to tremble.

"Look out," whispered Mimsy Borogrove, stepping back. "He's going to blow!"

Everyone else backed away, too.

Blork closed his eyes and took ten deep breaths. The tantrum faded.

Appus Meko looked deeply disappointed.

"Honest-to-Splat, Modra Ploogsik!" whispered Blork. "I didn't do it."

The teacher looked as if she wanted to believe him but was having a hard time doing so. "Any more mischief and I'll have to send you back to the bus, Blork," she said—which wasn't quite blaming him but was close enough to really hurt.

Blork felt rotten. But he didn't have any way to prove that he wasn't the one who had done it. And he knew that because he had pulled so many terrible tricks back in his brat days when something like this happened, everyone just assumed he was the culprit.

As soon as he could, Blork wandered away from the others so he could calm down. He found a little room and went in.

The only thing in the room was a machine labeled COPY MAKER. Blork wondered why the Museum of New Inventions had a copy machine. They had been around for centuries. Finally he decided it must be something the museum people used for their work.

The copy machine was made of polished metal. When Blork saw his reflection in the side of it, he said, "My, what a cranky face *you* have today, young man." (This was what the Childkeeper had said to him almost every morning since he had been hatched.) Then he stuck out his tongue.

The reflection stuck out its tongue, too.

Blork made the worst face he could think

of, a face that showed how really, really mad he was.

It looked so awful he decided to make a copy of it. He climbed onto the machine, lifted the cover, and plopped facedown on the glass. After closing his eyes so the light would not hurt them, he reached over and pushed the START button.

To Blork's surprise, no light came on. He was about to get up to see what was wrong when the top of the machine flipped over, dropping him inside. It was dark.

"Hey!" he cried. "What's going on here?"

The machine began to hum.

Strange things brushed across Blork's skin. Mechanical hands picked him up and shook him. He was tickled, poked, and prodded. Something wet and sticky slithered into his ear.

Then one of the mechanical hands shoved Blork's face into a pile of goop that felt like a giant mud pie.

"Help!" he cried. "Get me out of here!"

Since his face was stuck in gooey stuff, the words came out as "Mmmmm! Gmmmm eeeee attta eeer!"

Blork was scared. He couldn't move. He couldn't *breathe*. Just when he thought his lungs were going to pop, the hand pulled him out of the goop.

Suddenly the entire machine was filled with a strange blue light that nearly blinded him.

Then darkness again. Before Blork could stop blinking, a door opened in the side of the machine. The mechanical hands gave him a shove, and he went flying back into the room.

The door closed.

The machine stopped humming.

Blork sat on the floor rubbing his butt, which hurt where he had landed on it.

A man came running into the room. "What are you doing here?" he yelled. "This room is not open to the public yet."

"I'm hiding," said Blork.

"Well, you'll have to hide somewhere else. And don't touch that machine! We haven't finished testing it."

"What's the big deal?" asked Blork. "It's just a copy machine."

The man snorted. "This is not *just* a copy machine. It is a Complete Copier. It makes an exact duplicate of anything we put in it. At least, we hope it will, once we figure out how to make it work."

The man looked at the machine again.

"Uh-oh! It's set on negative. Good thing you didn't try to copy anything!"

Reaching over, he moved a big switch from NEGATIVE to POSITIVE.

Blork said nothing. He stared at the machine, wondering if anything would come out of it. But the machine just sat there, not making a sound.

Blork began to feel a little better.

The man put a hand on his shoulder and pushed him out the door.

Neither of them looked back.

So neither of them saw what came out of the machine as they were leaving the room.

3

KROLB

"I feel funny," said Blork as they were getting in the rocketbus to go back to the school.

"Makes sense," said Appus Meko. "You look funny, too."

Blork felt as if he should get angry. Somehow, it didn't seem to matter.

Modra Ploogsik took care of the situation for him. "I've had enough of your nonsense for one day," she said to Appus Meko. Then she plopped a Bubble of Silence over his head.

He shouted in protest, but, of course, no one could hear him.

"Best money I ever spent," said Modra Ploogsik, folding up the bag from the museum gift shop.

Now Blork felt like he should be happy. Yet somehow this didn't seem to matter, either.

Modra Ploogsik looked at him with concern. "Maybe you should go see the nurse when we get back to school," she said.

The nurse's dials blinked and whirred. "You feel a little cool," it told him. "I think you should lie down."

Blork stayed in the nurse's office for over an hour. When he went back to the classroom, Modra Ploogsik yelled at him for making faces through the window.

"I didn't make any faces," said Blork.

"You most certainly did!" said Modra Ploogsik. "Everyone in this class saw you."

Blork started to protest. Then he saw Modra Ploogsik's hand sliding across her desk. If he wasn't careful, she would pull the lever that would drop him into the Big Black Pit. He always hated it when he got sent there.

He went to his desk and sat quietly. To his surprise, he didn't feel angry, just a little tired.

After school Moomie Peevik, who looked like her old self again, thanked him for pulling her away from the Fat Injector.

Before Blork could think of what to say, Bob the Foreign Student went running by. He was crying.

"What's wrong, Bob?" called Blork.

"You should know, you rotten brat!"

Blork's eyes went wide. Despite the newsies naming him Space Brat, he had been trying like crazy *not* to be a brat ever since he got back from the Unexplored Zone. Why would Bob call him one now?

"What do you mean?" he shouted. He started to run after Bob, but he didn't seem to have the energy he needed to really chase him.

It didn't matter; Bob turned and threw a wadded-up ball of paper at Blork.

"What does it say?" asked Moomie Peevik.

Blork uncrumpled the paper. On it was a mean drawing of Bob. An arrow pointing at his head was labeled MISSING ANTENNA. Another arrow pointed to the middle of his face. This one was labeled GIANT HONKER!

"What a nasty, rotten picture!" cried Moomie Peevik.

Blork nodded. But he didn't say anything, because he recognized the style of the drawing.

Only one kid in their class drew that way: him!

The problem was, *he* hadn't drawn the picture.

Blork felt a little shiver run down his back.

When Blork got back to the Block 78 Child House, the Childkeeper met him at the door. Blork could tell from the way its eyes were glowing that he was in trouble.

Mimsy Borogrove stood behind the Childkeeper. She had tear marks running down her cheeks.

"Blork," said the Childkeeper sternly, "did you do this?"

"Do what?" asked Blork, feeling nervous.

"Show him," said the Childkeeper.

Mimsy Borogrove stepped out from behind the Childkeeper. She was holding a little basket. In it were three gitzels, the tiny furry animals that she kept as pets. (Usually kids were only allowed one pet, but gitzels were so small that a kid could keep three of them.)

Two of the gitzels looked as they always did. The third was bright blue, and its fur stuck out in all directions. When it saw Blork it went, "Niener niener niener!"—which is the sound a gitzel makes when it is afraid.

"I didn't do anything!" said Blork. But with the gitzel acting that way, he didn't think anyone was going to believe him.

Moomie Peevik looked at him in disgust. She didn't have a pet of her own yet—she said she was holding out for something unique— and she was very sensitive about the way people treated animals.

Feeling terrible, Blork headed for his room. Lakka shoved him as he walked by.

"Hey!" cried Blork. "What did you do that for?"

"As if you didn't know," sneered Lakka.

Blork felt rotten. But the worst was yet to come. That happened when he went into his room, and Lunk yelped in fear and tried to hide under the bed.

He didn't fit, of course. Normally the sight of the poodnoobie's big purple butt sticking in the air while he tried to climb under the bed would have made Blork laugh out loud. Now it only made him sad.

Even his own pet was afraid of him.

What was going on around here?

As he crawled into his bed, the scariest thing of all happened. Blork saw himself in the window! He blinked, rubbed his eyes, and looked again. The face was still there. For a moment he thought it must be his reflection. But the face looking in at him was upside down. Not only that, it was smiling—which he certainly was not at the moment.

Blork scrambled across the bed. But by the

time he got to the window, the face was gone.

Lunk whined.

Blork shivered.

He thought he knew what was going on, and he didn't like it.

What Blork thought was this: When he had fallen into the "Complete Copier" at the Museum of New Inventions, it had made a copy

of him—a *negative* copy. That copy had done all the things Blork was getting in trouble for.

The fact that Blork himself had played so many rotten tricks in the past made it easy for people to believe he was still doing them.

"I *hate* getting blamed for things I didn't do," said Blork with a sigh.

Lunk looked at him nervously.

Blork wondered if it was safe to go to sleep. What if his evil twin decided to sneak into his room and get rid of him so that *it* would be the only Blork?

He sat up and stared at the window.

Then he stared at the door.

He stared at the window again.

If his twin decided to visit, which way would he come in?

Blork decided he should stay awake all night, just in case.

It wasn't easy. He had been feeling tired and weak ever since he got out of the copy machine. He wondered if it had actually taken something out of him.

Finally Blork could stay awake no longer.

"Guard the door, Lunk," he said as he began to doze off.

He had not been asleep more than five minutes when the door opened and someone slipped into the room.

Lunk jumped onto the bed and began to whine.

Opening his eyes, Blork found himself staring into his own face.

"I must be dreaming," he muttered.

The Blork standing beside the bed laughed. "My name is Krolb," he said. "And I'm no dream. I'm your worst nightmare!"

4

SWAMP

Blork sat up straight. Lunk hid his head under three of his paws, then peeked out, looking back and forth between Blork and Krolb. Finally he jumped off the bed and put his head in a corner, where he couldn't see anything at all.

"You scared Lunk!" said Blork, not mentioning that he was pretty frightened himself.

"Good!" leered Krolb.

"Good?" asked Blork in surprise. "How can

anyone think it's good to scare a pood-noobie?"

"What you love, I hate," said Krolb. "What you hate, I love."

"You're my opposite?" asked Blork.

"I am not."

"You are too," replied Blork, more sure of himself now.

"Am not."

"Are too."

"Am not!"

"That's right, you're *not*," said Blork suddenly.

"I am too!" snapped Krolb.

"That's what I said!" cried Blork triumphantly.

Krolb looked upset. "Don't think it will always be that easy!" he said. Then he ran for the door.

"Wait," said Blork. "Come back!"

Krolb opened the door.

Suddenly Blork realized his mistake. "Go away!" he cried.

But Krolb had already left. So it was too late to get him to come back by trying to make him go away.

Blork stared at the door for a while. Then he patted the bed. "Come here, Lunk," he called. "Come here, boy."

But Lunk kept his head in the corner. Life was less confusing that way.

At breakfast the next morning the kids were all talking about a shocking news report: someone had stolen the Atomic Miniaturizer from the Museum of New Inventions.

The news made Blork nervous. But before he could think of what to do about it, the Childkeeper rolled in and started to yell at

him for snitching fried skunjies from the kitchen.

"I didn't do it," said Blork. "It was my evil twin, Krolb."

When the other kids finally stopped laughing, the Childkeeper whirred, "Blork, that is the most ridiculous excuse I have heard since the day they installed my ears. Keep it up and you may find yourself taking a trip to the Whacking Room."

Blork bit down on his tongue. He knew if he kept talking, he would only get in more trouble.

To his surprise, he didn't feel angry, just a little sad. Yesterday he would have had to work really hard not to have a tantrum over something like this. Now he just sighed.

"Blork, are you all right?" asked the Childkeeper. It sounded puzzled.

"No."

"What's wrong?"

Blork sighed again. What was wrong was that he had an evil twin named Krolb who was going around doing things that were getting him in trouble. What was even more wrong was that if he *told* the Childkeeper what was wrong, he would just get in more trouble for lying.

"Blork, what's wrong?" repeated the Childkeeper.

"Nothing," said Blork, knowing that if Krolb were here, he would automatically say, "Everything!"

In this case Krolb would be right.

Because it was Freeday, the kids did not have to go to school. Blork and Lunk went outside. Lunk was drooling and burping happily. He was feeling safe with Blork again, partly because poodnoobies can't remember things for very long.

At the back of the Block 78 Child House, Blork spotted a half-eaten skunjie. "Look, Lunk," he said. "A clue!"

Lunk stuck out his middle tongue and slurped up the skunjie.

"Hey!" yelled Blork. "How can I prove Krolb exists if you eat the evidence?"

Lunk drooled some more. Then he began sniffing around for another skunjie.

Blork smiled. "Good idea, boy. See if you can find his trail."

Though Lunk was not very smart, he was very good at tracking food. He began to follow the scent of the skunjies.

Blork followed Lunk.

Every once in a while Lunk would stop and sniff. Sometimes he would lick the ground.

Blork wasn't sure, but he thought the poodnoobie was licking up skunjie crumbs.

A half hour later Blork was getting nervous. He could see where they were heading, and he didn't like it.

"Lunk," he said, "if we keep going this way, we're going to end up in the Bubbling Swamp!"

Lunk licked the ground, burped, and kept going.

Blork didn't want to go into the Bubbling Swamp. It was filled with places where you could sink and never climb out. It was filled with plants that did strange things. It was filled with bad smells. And it was filled with big animals, like geezers, whiffles, and pewpits.

Worst of all, it was the home of the ferocious giant fuzzygrumper.

When he thought about it, Blork realized that it made sense that the Bubbling Swamp was where he would find Krolb. After all, if it was the last place on Splat that Blork wanted to go, then it was the most likely place for his reverse-everything twin to hide.

Lunk kept sniffing for skunjies.

Blork kept following Lunk.

They passed the big signs that said DANGER and OFF-LIMITS.

Soon they had entered the Bubbling Swamp.

Neither of them had noticed the person trailing close behind them.

Tiny bugs hummed and buzzed around Blork's head, nipping at his antennae. Strange cries drifted down from the trees where jeebers and cretzel birds lurked. A brown root from a bittersnip plant slithered out of the

murky water and tried to wrap itself around Blork's ankle.

Lunk followed Krolb's trail along squishy paths, past huge, vine-draped trees where little creatures skittered up and down the bark. He followed it to a soggy, boggy mud splat, where they had to jump from one stone to another to get across. (As he hopped from stone to stone, Blork remembered that Splat had gotten its name because the first spaceship of colonists to arrive on the planet had landed with a giant *splat!*)

Once Blork saw a giant eyeball staring at him out of the mud. Another time he saw a flock of seerses swinging through the trees by their long ears. Shortly afterward a fat grobutt waddled across the path.

Blork was not surprised. Modra Ploogsik had taught them that whenever you saw a seers, you were apt to see a grobutt, too.

Finally Lunk stopped in front of a cave. He stared at the dark opening and began to whine.

Blork stared at the opening, too. Should he go in?

Or was Krolb planning some kind of trap for him?

While he was trying to decide whether to enter the cave, someone stepped up from behind and tapped him on the shoulder.

"Yow!" cried Blork, spinning around.

Then he saw who it was.

His eyes went wide with surprise.

"What are *you* doing here?" he demanded.

5

CAVE

It was Moomic Pccvik. "I thought you might need help," she said. "So I followed you." She looked excited, worried, and frightened all at once.

Blork didn't know what to say. He did need help, but he didn't particularly want it to come from Moomie Peevik. He certainly didn't want Rugrub and Appus Meko to start making kissing sounds whenever they saw him.

"Remember, you saved me from the Fat Injector. So it's a fair trade."

While Blork was trying to figure out how to answer this, she added, "So—what's going on with you, anyway?"

Blork glanced at the cave, then bent his right antenna to indicate that they should move away from the opening before saying anything else.

Moomie Peevik nodded and followed Blork.

Lunk continued to crouch in front of the cave, staring into the darkness. His nose was quivering, and his middle tongue hung out of the side of his mouth.

Talking softly, Blork told Moomie Peevik everything that had happened since he threw himself onto the copy machine. While he talked, a squeazil slithered over his feet.

"So this kid Krolb isn't real?" asked Moomie Peevik as Blork tried to clean squeazil slime off his shoes.

"He's real enough to get me in a pile of trouble."

"But he's really just part of *you*, right?"

Blork wiggled his antennae. "What do you mean?"

"Well, do you feel like part of you is missing?"

"I feel kind of tired," admitted Blork. "Like some of my energy is gone."

"Well, there you are. That machine took something out of you. You have to think up some way to get it back."

"Now, how am I supposed to do that?" asked Blork in exasperation.

"How should I know?" yelled Moomie Peevik. "Do you expect me to figure out everything?"

"Shhhhh! I don't want him to hear us."

Moomie Peevik nodded. "All right," she whispered. "What else do we know about this guy?"

"Just that he does everything the opposite of me."

"Sort of like Beemer Pimbo," said Moomie Peevik.

Beemer Pimbo was the hero of a nursery rhyme every kid on Splat learned within a year of being hatched. It went:

Beemer Pimbo wouldn't do
Anything you told him to.
If you asked him to be good,
He'd hit you with a block of wood.
If you begged him to be quiet,
He would go and start a riot.
But when you cried, "Oh, just be *bad!*"
He was a perfect little lad.

Moomie Peevik recited it, then said, "Beemer Pimbo was a contrarian. That means he did the opposite of what you wanted—just like your twin."

"So if I want other people to know Krolb exists, I should say I want to keep him a secret!" said Blork excitedly.

"Makes sense to me," said Moomie Peevik.

"Come on," said Blork. He led the way to the cave. Putting his hand on top of Lunk's head, he shouted, "Krolb, you stay in there!"

Krolb strolled out of the cave, a big grin on his face.

"I just wanted to tell you that I've decided you should stay a secret," said Blork.

He expected Krolb to say, "Then I'm going to tell everyone I exist." Or maybe even just run off and do it. Instead, Krolb turned around and started back toward the cave.

"Hey," said Blork. "Where are you going?"

"Into my cave."

"Aren't you going to go tell people that you exist?"

"Do you think I'm as stupid as you are?" asked Krolb with a smirk.

"Well, you should be," said Blork before he realized what he was saying. "I mean . . ."

"I know what you're trying to do," said Krolb. "You want people to find out I exist, so you're trying to make me think you want the opposite. But remember, I know how you think because I think the same way."

"Only backward," said Moomie Peevik.

"Which is why I *really* don't like *you*," said Krolb.

Moomie Peevik blinked. Her face squinched up. For a minute she looked as if she was going to cry. Then, suddenly, her eyes went wide, and she started to smile.

"Blork!" she cried. "You care!"

Blork buried his face in his hands. "You are such a *bigmouth!*" he hissed at Krolb.

Krolb laughed and went back into the cave.

Blork followed him. When he entered the cave, he gasped in horror.

"I knew it!" he cried. "I knew you must have been the one who stole the Atomic Miniaturizer Ray Gun."

"I didn't steal it," said Krolb. "I just borrowed it for a while."

"Why?"

Krolb smiled. "Well," he said casually, "you've been so *good* for the last few weeks I feel a need to do something really rotten to make up for it."

"Like what?" asked Blork nervously.

Krolb shrugged. "I don't know. Shrink the whole city, maybe. Something like that."

"You wouldn't!" cried Blork.

"I would!" whispered Krolb.

"You mustn't!" whispered Blork.

"I must!" shouted Krolb.

"You're horrible," said Blork.

"I know," smirked Krolb. "And I got it all from you."

Blork hated that idea.

"You hate that idea, don't you?" asked Krolb happily. He picked up the Miniaturizer and pointed it at Blork. "I think you'd better go now," he said. "I have to make my plans."

Blork felt like having a tantrum, only he didn't have the energy for it. So he left the cave. It was either that, or get shrunk.

* * *

Blork and Moomie Peevik were sitting on a rock, staring at the cave. Lunk was nearby, sniffing around for skunjies.

"I think we should go," said Moomie Peevik. "He's not going to do anything now."

"How do you know that?" asked Blork.

"Well, Krolb does the opposite of what you want. But since you don't know what you want to do right now, he can't do the opposite of it."

"I think that makes sense," said Blork uncertainly.

"Of course it does. Come on."

"But what happens when we get back?" asked Blork. "Since I don't want him to come back with us, he probably will."

"Shhhhh!" said Moomie Peevik. "Don't say anything out loud."

"It doesn't matter. I think he can read my mind."

Moomie Peevik wrinkled her nose. "That's creepy!"

Before Blork could answer, he heard a terrible noise.

He smelled a terrible smell.

Looking up, he saw a terrible sight.

A giant orange fuzzygrumper was heading right for them.

"Run for your life!" cried Blork as the fuzzygrumper knocked over a tree.

It was too late. The fuzzygrumper was there. Reaching out with one giant hand, it scooped up Lunk. Reaching out with its other giant hand, it scooped up Moomie Peevik.

Then it went squishing off through the swamp.

6

FUZZY-GRUMPER

Blork went running back to the cave. "Krolb! Krolb!" he cried. "You have to help me! A giant fuzzygrumper just kidnapped Lunk and Moomie Peevik."

Krolb laughed in Blork's face. "Why should I care?"

"I can't believe this," said Blork. "Stop acting like that! We have to save them!"

Krolb leaned against the wall of the cave and yawned. "If you want to save them, go save them. If *you* want to go, *I* want to stay here."

"All right," said Blork. "Stay here! I don't want your help anyway!"

He was so mad he really meant it.

"Fine," said Krolb, jumping to his feet. "Let's go!"

Blork blinked. "You mean you're coming?"

"Of course."

"That's great!" cried Blork.

"Forget it," said Krolb. "I'm staying. Get out of here."

In the distance Blork heard Moomie Peevik screaming. He heard Lunk howling in fear. Blork was in a panic. Krolb was leaning against the cave wall again, looking as if he was about to take a nap.

Lunging forward, Blork grabbed the Atomic Miniaturizer Ray Gun.

"Hey!" cried Krolb. "Give that back!"

Blork didn't even answer. Racing out of the cave, he headed after the fuzzygrumper.

It was not hard to follow the fuzzygrumper's trail. Blork raced along the path of broken plants. Once he fell into one of the fuzzygrumper's footprints. Another time he sank up to his waist in swamp muck. But he kept going because he had to save Lunk and Moomie Peevik.

Krolb was running along behind him, shouting, "You bring that back!"

"Get away from me!" cried Blork, which only made Krolb run faster. Suddenly he tackled Blork. The two of them fell into a mudhole.

"Gotcha!" cried Krolb.

"Help!" cried Moomie Peevik, off in the distance. Lunk was still howling in terror.

"Let me go!" shouted Blork. "I have to go help them."

"You're not going anywhere," said Krolb.

Suddenly a great rage began to bubble inside Blork. He began to shake. He began to shiver. His entire body began to tremble.

And then it happened.

Blork had a tantrum.

Not just any tantrum.

He had what may just possibly have been the greatest tantrum in the history of the galaxy—even greater than the tantrum he had thrown the day the Mighty Squat had threatened to eat Lunk.

"I CAN'T BELIEVE IT!" screamed Blork, throwing himself on the ground. "I CAN'T BELIEVE YOU ARE SUCH A ROTTEN, GREEDY, DISGUSTING, CONTRARY, BEEMER PIMBO OF A SPLATOON, AND THAT YOU CAME FROM ME! I AM SO DISGUSTED I COULD EXPLODE!"

And indeed, Blork looked as if he was on the verge of exploding as he burst out of Krolb's arms and began bouncing off the trees.

Swamp creatures began to howl in fear. Vines rolled into the trees to take shelter. Insects fell out of the air in astonishment. The swamp itself stopped bubbling.

And in the mudhole something strange was happening. The wilder Blork's tantrum got, the nicer Krolb began to act.

"Don't be so upset," he said at first.

"DON'T TALK TO ME!" screamed Blork.

"No, I mean it. I'm not mad or anything," said Krolb.

"OF COURSE YOU'RE NOT MAD!" roared Blork, who was rolling around in the

mud in his fury. "I'M MAD, SO YOU'RE FEELING NICE. WELL, THAT'S . . . JUST . . . *SWELL!*"

Krolb began to cry. Big tears rolled down his green cheeks. "You don't understand," he said. "I feel this great surge of sweetness in me. I want to make the world all better. I want to make everyone happy. I want to help you, Blork."

"*AAAAAAARRRRRGGGGGHHHHHH!*" cried Blork, turning three different shades of blue.

Krolb ran over and threw his arms around his twin. "Let me hug you!" he cried. "Maybe then you'll feel better."

"LEAVE ME ALONE!" cried Blork.

Krolb threw his arms around him.

"I HATE YOU!" cried Blork. "GO AWAY! GO AS FAR AWAY AS YOU CAN!"

"I love you!" whispered Krolb, hugging Blork even tighter. "I want to get as close to you as I can."

Suddenly a ring of blue light surrounded the two boys—the same blue light that had filled the Complete Copier. Blork's skin began to tingle. His ears began to ring. Before he knew what was happening, Krolb was gone.

Blinking in surprise, Blork put his hand on his chest. He felt like his old self again, not half here and half gone, not half this and half that.

"This is *great!*" cried Blork.

His happiness lasted about three seconds. Then a distant scream reminded him that Lunk and Moomie Peevik were still in big trouble.

Snatching up the Atomic Miniaturizer, he began to run.

At last he came to the fuzzygrumper's lair.

It was a terrifying sight: a swampy grotto where the great orange fuzzygrumper sat holding Moomie Peevik in one furry hand and Lunk in the other.

The beast was looking from hand to hand, its enormous tongue lobbing in and out of its mouth. Blork got the feeling it was trying to decide whether to eat Lunk or Moomie Peevik first. He had to shrink the thing, and he had to do it fast.

But he couldn't use the Atomic Miniaturizer while the fuzzygrumper was still holding its victims. That would shrink them, too. And there was no way to make them big again.

He had to get the fuzzygrumper to drop them. But the only way he could think of to do that was to get it interested in him, instead.

The idea was scary. What if he didn't have time to use the Miniaturizer?

What if it didn't work on fuzzygrumpers?

What if . . .

Blork swallowed. The *what ifs* didn't make any difference. He had to try.

"Hey, fuzzygrumper!" he yelled. "Why don't you pick on someone your own size?"

"Aroonga?" snorted the fuzzygrumper.

"You heard me!" yelled Blork. "Put them down and pick on someone your own size."

"Ernna Bernna Blamma!" roared the fuzzygrumper. But it didn't let go of Lunk and Moomie Peevik.

"I said *let them go!*" cried Blork, running up to the fuzzygrumper and jumping on its foot with all his weight—which wasn't easy, since the foot was so big.

"*Arooonga Boonga Boonga!*" screamed the fuzzygrumper. Dropping Lunk and Moomie Peevik, it reached for Blork.

"Run!" Blork yelled to Lunk and Moomie Peevik.

"Run!" Moomie Peevik yelled to Blork and Lunk.

Lunk began to run. Unfortunately, he ran in circles, which didn't do much to get him away from the fuzzygrumper.

It didn't make any difference. The fuzzygrumper's attention was all on Blork. Reaching down with its great furry arms, it tried to grab him.

Blork ran. He had to find a place where he could stop to use the Miniaturizer. He tripped and fell in a bubbling mudhole. The fuzzygrumper loomed above him. Blork got the Miniaturizer in position and pulled the trigger.

Nothing happened.

Blork stared at the Miniaturizer in horror. The end of it was clogged with swamp slime.

7

HERO

The fuzzygrumper's hand was about to close around Blork when Moomie Peevik jumped onto the back of its huge leg.

"Leave him alone, you big hairy meatball!" she screamed. Then she sank her teeth into its skin.

Roaring with anger, the fuzzygrumper spun around, trying to grab Moomie Peevik. Instead, it tripped over Lunk, who was still galloping in circles and yelping with fear.

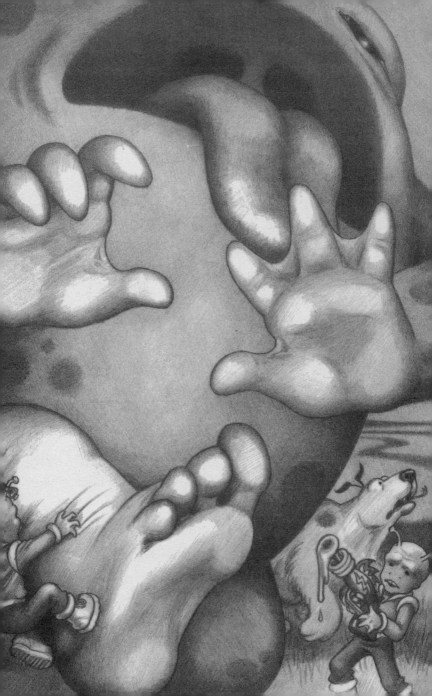

"Aroonga Boonga *Boo-o-o-o-oonga!*" cried the fuzzygrumper as it fell.

A great wave of swamp water rolled over Blork, washing the swamp slime from the end of the Miniaturizer.

"Out of the way, everyone!" cried Blork. "Out of the way!"

Moomie Peevik skittled in one direction. Lunk went racing in the other.

The furious fuzzygrumper was crawling toward Blork. It was extending one huge, orange paw to grab him when Blork lifted the Miniaturizer and fired.

A crackling, zapping sound filled the air.

A purple cloud of loose atoms began to form over the fuzzygrumper as it shrank . . . and shrank . . . and shrank . . . until it barely came up to Blork's knee.

"Aroonga Boonga Boonga!" it whimpered in a tiny voice.

"It's kind of cute that size," said Moomie Peevik, coming up behind Blork. "And it's certainly unique. Do you think the Childkeeper would let me have it for a pet?"

"You know the rule," said Blork. "Every kid can have one pet. At least the Childkeeper can't complain that this one will get bigger," he added, remembering what the Childkeeper had said the day he came home with Lunk.

Moomie Peevik knelt and looked at the fuzzygrumper.

"Aroonga Boonga Boonga!" it screamed.

She poked it gently in the tummy with her finger.

It started to laugh. Soon it was laughing so hard that it fell over.

"It's ticklish!" said Moomie Peevik.

"We'd better go," said Blork. "For all we know, there may be another one around here."

Tucking the Atomic Miniaturizer under his arm, Blork led the way out of the swamp.

Moomie Peevik picked up the tiny fuzzygrumper, which was still giggling helplessly. Tucking it under her arm, she followed Blork.

Lunk came galumphing along behind them.

*   *   *

Appus Meko was the first to see them coming. He immediately started making kissy noises against the back of his hand.

For an instant Blork considered trying to miniaturize his enemy. Part of him wanted to; another part of him said that it would be a bad idea. Blork felt like there was a war going on inside of him—a war between Blork and Krolb.

Finally he put down the Miniaturizer. "Moomie Peevik is my friend!" he shouted. "So just shut your blubbering mouth-hole, Appus Meko, before I kiss you myself!"

Appus Meko turned and ran as fast as he could.

Moomie Peevik looked a little confused but didn't say anything.

When they took the Atomic Miniaturizer Ray Gun to the Childkeeper, it began to roll in circles, buzzing and whirring and making "Red Alert!" noises.

"Danger, danger, danger!" it shrieked. "Clear the house! Clear the house!"

Blork had never seen the Childkeeper panic

before. He put the Atomic Miniaturizer Ray Gun on the floor and backed away from it.

"Aren't you going to try to shrink us?" asked the Childkeeper.

Blork felt terrible that the Childkeeper would even think he might do such a thing.

Then he remembered how he had felt about Appus Meko just a few seconds ago.

"I might think about it," he said. "But I would never do something like that."

"Then why did you steal this from the museum?" asked the Childkeeper, pointing to the Atomic Miniaturizer Ray Gun.

"*I* didn't steal it!" cried Blork. "*Krolb* did!"

"Now, Blork," said the Childkeeper, "I don't want you to start that nonsense. . . ."

"It's true!" said Moomie Peevik. "I saw the whole thing!"

Then she told everything that had happened.

Moomie Peevik had to tell the whole story over and over again, first to Modra Ploogsik, then to the Mayor, and finally to the Big Boss of Splat.

Everyone decided that Blork was a hero.

Soon his picture was everywhere. "SPACE BRAT" SAVES CITY FROM SHRINKING! read the headlines. He was interviewed by all the major newsies. Producers wanted to buy the rights to his life story.

Blork was happy.

Lunk was happy.

Moomie Peevik and her new pet fuzzy-grumper were happy.

But Appus Meko was so mad he didn't say anything to Blork for three weeks.

That would have been enough reward for Blork as it was. But one day the Big Boss of Splat called and said that he wanted to give him a medal.

"Could I have a space scooter instead?" asked Blork.

The Big Boss thought about it for a few minutes. Finally he said, "I guess a hero like you can have just about anything he wants."

When the space scooter arrived the next day, Blork was thrilled, the Childkeeper was nervous, and Appus Meko was furious. "I can't believe it!" he said. "I can't believe Blork gets a space scooter. I should get to share it. Heck, the whole thing never would have happened if Blork hadn't gotten so mad at the Museum of New Inventions. And that wouldn't have happened if I hadn't plugged Moomie Peevik into . . ."

He stopped. His cheeks turned dark green.

"Go on," said Moomie Peevik. "Finish what you were saying."

"Nothing," said Appus Meko desperately. "I wasn't saying anything."

Moomie Peevik put her fuzzygrumper on the ground. "Get him!" she said, pointing at Appus Meko.

"Aroonga Boonga Boonga!" cried the fuzzy-grumper.

Even a tiny fuzzygrumper can be terrifying when it takes after someone. Soon Appus Meko was running toward the Block 78 Child House, screaming, "Help! Help! Somebody help me!"

Moomie Peevik sighed. "I suppose I'd better go save him," she said. "Then I want to have a little talk with the Childkeeper."

Chuckling to herself, she started after Appus

Meko and the fuzzygrumper. But despite Appus Meko's cries for help, she went very, *very* slowly, as if she had all the time in the world.

Blork climbed into the space scooter. "Come on, Lunk," he said, patting the seat next to him. "Let's try this baby out!"

Lunk climbed in. Blork closed the top and pressed START. Seconds later they were heading for the stratosphere.

"Watch out, Splat!" he cried. "Blork has got his wings. Space Brat and awaaaaay!"

Lunk licked his face and burped happily.

About the Author and the Illustrator

BRUCE COVILLE was born in Syracuse, New York. He grew up in a rural area north of the city, around the corner from his grandparents' dairy farm. In the years before he was able to make his living full-time as a writer, Bruce was, among other things, a gravedigger, a toymaker, a magazine editor, and a door-to-door salesman. He loves reading, musical theater, and being outdoors.

In addition to more than sixty books for young readers, Bruce has written poems, plays, short stories, newspaper articles, thousands of letters, and several years' worth of journal entries.

Some of Bruce's best-known books are *My Teacher Is an Alien*, *Goblins in the Castle*, and *Aliens Ate My Homework*.

KATHERINE COVILLE is a self-taught artist who is known for her ability to combine finely detailed drawings with a deliciously wacky sense of humor. She is also a toymaker, specializing in creatures hitherto unseen on this planet. Her other collaborations with Bruce Coville include *The Monster's Ring*, *The Foolish Giant*, *Sarah's Unicorn*, *Goblins in the Castle*, *Aliens Ate My Homework*, and the *Space Brat* series.

The Covilles live in a brick house in Syracuse along with their youngest child, three cats, and a jet-powered Norwegian elkhound named Thor.